First published in Great Britain in 1994 by
The Bodley Head Children's Books

This edition published in Great Britain and in the USA in 2008 by
Frances Lincoln Children's Books, 4 Torriano Mews,
Torriano Avenue, London NW5 2RZ
www.franceslincoln.com

British Library Cataloguing in Publication Data
available on request

ISBN 978-1-84507-724-2

Printed in Singapore

9 8 7 6 5 4 3 2 1

DOING CHRISTMAS

Sarah Garland

F

FRANCES LINCOLN
CHILDREN'S BOOKS

Granny is coming for Christmas.

We will do the shopping,

and boil the pudding,

and dig up the tree,

And get everything ready
for Christmas.

It is Christmas Day and here comes Granny.

She is early.

She has brought some presents.

Granny tells stories

until lunchtime.

Then we walk to the park.

It is time to say goodbye.

It is the end of Christmas day.